# A Rabbit for Easter

by **Carol Carrick** pictures by **Donald Carrick**

GREENWILLOW BOOKS
A Division of William Morrow & Company, Inc., New York

LIBRARY OF CONGRESS CATALOGING IN PUBLICATION DATA
Carrick, Carol.    A rabbit for Easter.    Summary: Paul is entrusted with the class rabbit over
Easter vacation.    [1.  Rabbits—Fiction.    2.  Easter stories]    I.  Carrick, Donald.    II.  Title.
PZ7.C2344Rab    [E]    78-15647    ISBN 0-688-80195-1    ISBN 0-688-84195-3 lib. bdg.

FOR FRANCES SAWYER

Paul liked kindergarten. He liked the playhouse with its bed and a sink to wash dishes. He liked to put on the headphones to listen to records. And there were enough blocks to build anything in the world. But the best thing of all in kindergarten was Sam, the rabbit.

As soon as Paul came to school in the morning, he went over to Sam's cage. He always found Sam standing on his hind legs, waiting for his treat. When it was Paul's turn to feed Sam, he carefully held the raisins, one by one, between his finger and thumb so Sam could take them from his hand. First Paul felt the tickley whiskers, then a gentle tug, and the raisin was gone. Next Paul filled Sam's dish with rabbit pellets and Mrs. Sawyer, the teacher, brought Sam fresh water.

When the children sat quietly on the rug at storytelling time, Sam was let out of the cage for his exercise. Hop, hop, he raced along the sides of the room. Hop, hop, through the doll's house. Hop, hop, behind the book rack and under the teacher's desk. His sharp claws slipped on the smooth tile floor and his hind feet flew out from under him when he skidded around corners.

Then Sam disappeared for a while, but the children knew where he was because they could hear the sound of cardboard tearing. Sam was under a table where some boxes were piled. He liked to chew on things.

Mrs. Sawyer put a carrot in Sam's cage before the children went out for recess. After Sam hopped back into his cage to eat it, someone shut the door and Mrs. Sawyer reminded them to push the hook down all the way so Sam could not get out. Sam had always lived in a cage and if he got lost, he might not know how to take care of himself.

Paul was the happiest boy in the class on the last day of school, because he was going to look after Sam during Easter vacation.

Paul's father came when school was over to help bring the rabbit home.

"Let's put his cage on top of the clothes dryer where we can see him," Paul's mother said as his father carried Sam's cage in from the car.

Paul's cat, Fluffy, wanted to see Sam, too. She jumped up on the cage and peered over the top. Sam huddled in a corner.

"Fluffy! Get down, you bad girl!" Paul clapped his hands to scare the cat away.

Paul invited Stacey and Ralph from next door to come over and meet Sam.

"Ooo," said Stacey. "He's nice."

"What can he do?" asked Ralph.

"He hops around," said Paul, "and you can pet him."

Paul showed them how he gently stroked Sam from his head to his tail, the way his fur grew. Sam sat still with his ears flattened and his eyes half closed. He liked being petted.

The next morning when Paul went into the kitchen for his breakfast, the rabbit was standing up in his cage.

"Look, Mom," Paul said, "Sam's waiting for his treat."

Paul fed Sam some raisins. Then he poured a cup of pellets into the rabbit's bowl and asked his mother for some water.

As Paul ate his breakfast, he watched Sam chew each mouthful sideways, the way rabbits eat. Sam looked very much at home.

Then Paul let Sam out for his exercise. The rabbit hopped under the dining room table. His nose wiggled and his ears turned toward every new sound. He hopped down the hall and explored the living room.

Sam had just come out from behind the couch and was nibbling on Paul's shoes, when there was a banging on the front door. Sam hid behind the couch again. Paul knew who knocked like that. It must be Ralph and Stacey.

"Paul, look what I got," Stacey said, when he opened the door. "A two-wheeler! And it's got training wheels so I can ride it."

Paul looked out on the sidewalk where the shiny new bicycle was parked.

"Do you want to try it?" Stacey asked.

Paul ran to get his coat. He had never been on a big bicycle before.

After Ralph helped him on the bike, Paul rode slowly up and down the street. Then Stacey wanted her bicycle back.

"Can I have another turn?" he asked.

"Later," she promised.

Paul watched her ride up and down. Every time she passed, he asked if he could have another ride. But Stacey always said, "Not yet." So he went home.

As soon as Paul opened the door, he remembered Sam. He had forgotten to put the rabbit back in his cage! Paul looked behind the couch. No Sam. He looked under all the chairs and the coffee table. No Sam. He looked in the hall and under the dining room table, but there was no rabbit.

Maybe his mother had put Sam back. Paul went into the kitchen. But the door of the cage was still open and there was no rabbit inside.

Paul's mother was upstairs making the beds.

"Mom," he said. "I can't find Sam. I've looked all over the house and he's gone."

"He's just hiding somewhere," she said. "Maybe he followed me upstairs."

Paul looked under all the beds, opened all the closet doors, and even looked in the bathtub. But he couldn't find Sam anywhere.

Now Paul was really worried. Maybe Sam had gotten out when the door was open. If he was outside, they would never find him. He thought of the rabbit wandering farther and farther away. Dogs might chase him. He might run in front of a car.

Paul ran downstairs to look in all the hiding places again. He had to find Sam right away.

"Oh, Sam, where are you?" Paul pleaded. How could he tell Mrs. Sawyer and the other children that he had lost their rabbit? He had promised to take good care of Sam. Paul didn't know what to do next.

Then he had a terrible thought. Fluffy! He must find Sam before
the cat did. Maybe Fluffy had gotten Sam already!

"Oh, no! Fluffy! Here, Fluffy!"

Paul ran to the back door and looked out. Fluffy was lying in the
sun on the garbage can cover. When she saw Paul, she jumped
down and ran to the door.

"You can't come in," he shouted and slammed the door.

It was then Paul heard the crunching sound coming from the corner of the kitchen where the washing machine was. There was a pile of dirty clothes on the floor next to the laundry basket. And in the basket, gnawing on the wicker sides, was Sam.

"Mother, I found Sam!" Paul shouted. "He's in the wash basket."

"Wonderful!" she called from upstairs. His mother came down and put Sam safely back in his cage. "Maybe he thought it was an Easter basket," she said.

Paul laughed. He was so happy that Sam was found.

After vacation Paul and Sam returned to school. When it was time for recess, a carrot was placed in Sam's cage and he hopped through the open door.

"Paul, would you shut the door to Sam's cage, please?" Mrs. Sawyer asked.

Paul went over to the cage and looked at Sam, who was chewing his carrot and watching Paul with one bright eye.

Paul had not told anyone that Sam had almost been lost, but when he locked the door of the cage, he was very careful to push the hook all the way down.